First published in the United States 1987 by
Dial Books for Young Readers
2 Park Avenue
New York, New York 10016

Published simultaneously in Canada by
Fitzhenry & Whiteside Limited, Toronto
Published in Great Britain by Methuen Children's Books Ltd.
Text copyright © 1987 by Moira Miller
Illustrations copyright © 1987 by Ian Deuchar
All rights reserved.
Printed in Great Britian
C O B E
First Edition
1 3 5 7 9 10 8 6 4 2

Library of Congress Cataloging in Publication Data
Miller, Moira. The proverbial mouse.
Summary: During his nightly quests for food in a toy shop,
a hungry mouse learns a number of proverbs
from the toys and eventually devises one himself
for the cat that tries to catch him.
[1. Mice—Fiction. 2. Toys—Fiction.]
I. Deuchar, Ian, ill. II. Title.
PZ7.M6313Pr 1987   [E]   86-16737
ISBN 0-8037-0195-0

The Proverbial Mouse

by MOIRA MILLER · pictures by IAN DEUCHAR

Dial Books for Young Readers · New York

In the middle of the night,
in the dark that follows light,
a Little Mouse stirred and stretched,
twitched his whiskers, and woke up.

"Bless me," said the Little Mouse.
"there is nothing to eat around this house.
My tum is empty, my toes are empty,
my tail is empty too."

He sharpened his toes, wiggled his nose,
and set out to hunt for food.

Out into the shop he crept.
All was quiet, all was still.
Only the dust danced in the moonlight.

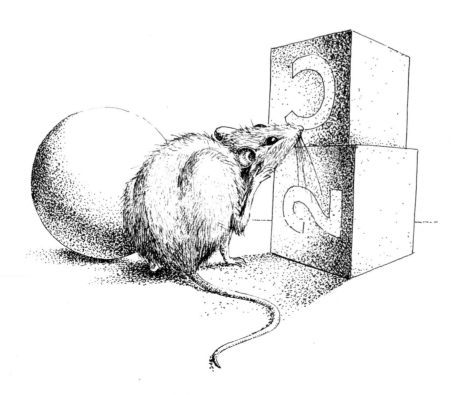

The Little Mouse was hungry.
He twitched his whiskers and sniffed around.
"Aha," he said, "what do I see?
Milk and apples just for me."

He sharpened his toes, wiggled his nose,
and scampered *whiskery-quick* onto the table.

But the milk and apples were not what they seemed to be.

"Look before you leap," said the Jack-in-the-Box.

The Little Mouse was still hungry.
He twitched his whiskers
and sniffed around.
"Oh-ho," he said, "what do I see?
A fine yellow cheese, just for me."

He sharpened his toes, wiggled his nose,
and tiptoed *tikki-tikki-tikki* along the table.

But the fine yellow cheese was not what it seemed to be.

"All that glitters is not gold," said the China Pig.

The Little Mouse was still more hungry.
He twitched his whiskers and sniffed around.
"Tee-hee," he said, "what do I see?
A sugar-iced cake, just for me."

He sharpened his toes, wiggled his nose,
and scampered *twist-whist* down the rope.

But the sugar-iced cake was not what what it seemed to be.
Rum-tee-tum-tum. He skipped a tune on the drum.

"You cannot have your cake and beat it,"
said the Wooden Soldier.

And still the Little Mouse was very hungry.
"So-ho," he said, "What do I see?
A basket of eggs, just for me."

He sharpened his toes, wiggled his nose,
and crept *tippety-click* across the floor.

But the basket of eggs was not what it seemed to be.

"Don't count your chickens before they hatch," said the Fluffy Bird.

The Little Mouse was hungrier than ever.
His tummy rumbled.
The Little Mouse grumbled.
"My tum is empty, my toes are empty,
my tail is empty too."

He danced a little Hungry Dance
    rickety-tickety-tickety-scritch
            on his four pink feet.

Under the counter, by his dish of milk,
the Marmalade Cat cocked an ear
and opened one green spy-eye.

He twitched a whisker, he stretched a claw —
a long, sharp claw.

His tummy rumbled, his little pink tongue
licked his lips.
Out he crept on four soft paws.

But still the Little Mouse danced his Hungry Dance
    rickety-tickety-tickety-scritch
            on his four pink feet.

The Cat pounced. The dish bounced.

Lickety-split, the Little Mouse
skipped up to a high shelf.

The Marmalade Cat snarled and spat,
his paws in a puddle, his fur all wet.

"No use crying over spilt milk,"
squeaked the Little Mouse
from the top of the shop.

"True," growled the Fat, Furry Brown Bear
on the shelf by his side.

The Little Mouse twitched his whiskers
and sniffed around.
"Aha," he said, "what do I see?
Bread and cheese — a feast for me."

He sharpened his toes, wiggled his nose,
and squeezed past the Fat, Furry Brown Bear.

And the bread and cheese were EXACTLY
what they seemed to be.

In the middle of the night, in the dark before the light,
the Little Mouse nibbled and nibbled until his tail was full,
his toes were full . . .

and his tum was very, very full.